Little Miss Middle

ISBN 978-1-6396-1014-3 (paperback)
ISBN 978-1-0980-8364-9 (hardcover)
ISBN 978-1-0980-8365-6 (digital)

Christian Faith Publishing, Inc.
832 Park Avenue
Meadville, PA 16335
www.christianfaithpublishing.com

Printed in the United States of America

Little Miss Middle

PATRICIA PENTECOST

One cold winter day, Jenny and her two sisters went to stay at Grandma's house. They had fun all day. Grandma took them to the library which was one of their favorite places and out to lunch.

When they got back to Grandma's house, they played dress up in Grandma's clothes, put on a fashion show, and played school at the old desk in the spare bedroom.

They all should have been very sleepy that night, but as Grandma lay across the bottom of the bed waiting for all the girls to fall asleep, Jenny's eyes stayed open. Jenny's sisters Jaclyn and Joanna fell asleep right away.

Grandma finally whispered, "Aren't you sleepy, Jenny?"

"No," answered Jenny.

Then Grandma got up, grabbed a big blanket, and said, "Come here, Jenny, let me rock you."

Jenny hopped out of bed and climbed unto Grandma's lap, in the big rocking chair next to the bed. Grandma wrapped the blanket around her, real snuggly.

As they rocked, Grandma asked Jenny, "Is something bothering you? You've been sort of quiet today."

Jenny didn't answer for a minute, then she said, "Sometimes I wish I was Jaclyn 'cause she's the biggest. She knows how to do everything real good, and she's always saying, 'I was the first one born.' She's thirteen already and gets to do a lot of things I don't."

"Oh, I see," said Grandma. "Is there anything else?"

Again, Jenny was quiet.

Then Grandma asked, "Do you ever wish you were Joanna?"

Joanna was the youngest. Five years old.

"Sometimes I wish I was Joanna. Everyone always says how cute she is, and she gets her own way lots of times," said Jenny.

"So," said Grandma, "Jaclyn's special 'cause she's the biggest, and Joanna is special 'cause she is the littlest. Isn't there anything special about being in the middle?"

"I don't think so," said Jenny.

"Well," said Grandma, "God says you're special, and I think you're special too. Let me tell you a story, Jenny."

Jenny loved Grandma's stories and snuggled up closer to listen. Grandma's stories usually started with once upon a time or one day...

Once upon a time, there was a little girl. She was nine years old, and her name was Suzie. Suzie's grandma always called her Little Miss Middle because she was in the middle of two other sisters, too, just like you.

Well, Suzie didn't like being in the middle either. Until one day, Grandma said, "Let's go for a walk, Suzie, and see if we can find anything special about being in the middle."

First, they walked through the park. They stopped to look at a flower garden. The flowers were beautiful, all different kinds, and all different colors.

Then Grandma said, "Look in the middle of the garden, Suzie, and tell me what you see."

Suzie looked and said, "An angel."

"Yes," said Grandma, "a beautiful angel statue, right in the middle. The middle must be very special place to be."

Suzie didn't say anything, but she got a little smile on her face as they walked on.

Soon Grandma and Suzie were walking past all the stores downtown. They stopped in front of the bakery. There, inside the window, was a beautiful wedding cake. White icing, with candy pearls, and little red candy roses all over it. At the very top stood two special little dolls. The bride and groom.

Grandma asked Suzie, "Where are the bride and groom on the cake?"

"On the top," said Suzie.

"But where on the top?" asked Grandma.

"In the middle, on the top," said Suzie with a big smile.

"Yes," said Grandma, "in the middle."

"And look," said Suzie, pointing to the chocolate cookies; the frosting is in the middle of those cookies. "The frosting is my favorite part! This is fun! Can we look for some more special things in the middle, Grandma?"

"Ok," chuckled Grandma.

Down the street on the corner was the church grandma and Suzie's family went to every Sunday. Grandma told Suzie they would find something very special, in the middle, in the church. Suzie tried to think of something she had seen that was special and in the middle, then she said, "I know, Grandma, the cross! The cross is special, and it's in the middle, on the stage."

"Yes," said Grandma, "that's very good thinking. The cross is very special, and it's in the middle. Buts there is something else that I'm thinking of."

"Tell me, Grandma, tell me," pleaded Suzie.

"I will tell you soon," said Grandma. "Let's go in first."

Pastor Dow was in the sanctuary when Grandma and Suzie went in. Grandma asked Pastor if he would pray a special blessing over Suzie, so she will always know how special she is. He prayed a beautiful prayer, and they thanked him.

Then Grandma said, "Let's sit down in the pew for a minute, Suzie, and I'll tell you what I was thinking of. Do you remember what Pastor said at the end of the prayer?"

"I'm not sure," said Suzie.

He said, "In the name of the Father and of the Son and of the Holy Spirit. Who did he say in the middle?"

"The Son," said Suzie. "He said the Son in the middle."

"That's right," said Grandma. "And who is the Son?"

"Jesus," said Suzie with a big smile.

Grandma smiled too and said, "You can't get any more special than Jesus in the middle. Right, Suzie?"

"Right, Grandma," said Suzie and they laughed and gave each other a big hug.

Then Grandma said, "We'd better start home now."

On their way home, Grandma said, "You look for some things now, Suzie."

Suzie looked and looked. Soon she said, "I can't find anything else in the middle, Grandma."

"You keep looking," said Grandma. "It takes practice."

They were walking past the TV store when Grandma said, "Look, Suzie, the Olympic ice-skaters are on television. They're going to announce the winners. Let's stop a minute and watch."

All at once, Suzie got all excited and said, "I see one! I see one!"

"You see one what?" said Grandma.

"I see someone special, in the middle! The best winner is in the middle!" shouted Suzie.

"That's right," said Grandma. "The winner is always in the middle."

Suzie and Grandma laughed and talked about all the things they saw as they walked on home. Suzie was sure feeling happier about herself and about being in the middle too as she skipped along.

"How did you like that story, Jenny?"

14

"I liked it, Grandma," said Jenny. "Tell it to me again."

Grandma chuckled and said, "Maybe tomorrow. Jenny, how does that story make you feel inside?"

"Warm and happy," said Jenny.

"Me too," said Grandma. "And if you ever start to feel like you're not as special 'cause you're not the biggest or the littlest, you just remember our story about Little Miss Middle."

"I will," said Jenny then she said, "I love you, Grandma. I'm glad I'm not the biggest, and I'm glad I'm not the littlest. I'm glad I'm in the middle."

Grandma said, "I love you too, Jenny, you'll always be my Little Miss Middle."

Grandma continued to rock Jenny quietly, and soon Jenny was fast asleep.

The next Sunday when the family went to church, the theme of the sermon was "In God's Eyes." The three sisters all sang beautifully and were singing together this Sunday.

They sang Love Lifted Me. "When nothing else could help, love lifted me."

Mama had made them dresses to match, and as they sang, the families in the pews all clapped and sang along.

Pastor DOW reminded, "God's people, God doesn't see firsts, seconds, or thirds. God doesn't see special or unspecial. God see's through eyes of love—we should all look through eyes of love and see as God does. We're all firsts in his eyes. We're all special in his eyes. We're all the same in God's eyes."

Everybody learned a big lesson that day, and Little Miss Middle never felt unspecial ever again.

The End

Grandma's Stories

With Love,
Gramma Storie

About the Author

Dear reader,

I chose this picture not because I have a tiara on but because it's my eightieth birthday. All my children and grandchildren are with me. Without them, I would not be me nor would there be any stories. They are my stories, they are my loves, thoughts, and prayers. God has been good to me. My stories are his love for all the children of the world.

I hope you like them; they are for you also.